FUN

JAN MARK

illustrated by Michael Foreman

VIKING KESTREL

For Emma and Isabel Cullingford

J.M.

VIKING KESTREL
Published by the Penguin Group
Viking Penguin Inc., 40 West 23rd Street, New York, New York 10010, U.S.A.
Penguin Books Ltd, 27 Wrights Lane, London W8 5TZ, England
Penguin Books Australia Ltd, Ringwood, Victoria, Australia
Penguin Books Canada Ltd, 2801 John Street, Markham, Ontario, Canada L3R 1B4
Penguin Books (N.Z.) Ltd, 182–190 Wairau Road, Auckland 10, New Zealand

Penguin Books Ltd, Registered Offices: Harmondsworth, Middlesex, England

First published in Great Britain by Victor Gollancz Ltd, 1987
First American Edition
Published in 1988

Text copyright © Jan Mark, 1987
Illustrations copyright © Michael Foreman, 1987

ISBN 0-670-82457-7

Printed in Hong Kong by Imago Publishing Limited

1 2 3 4 5 92 91 90 89 88

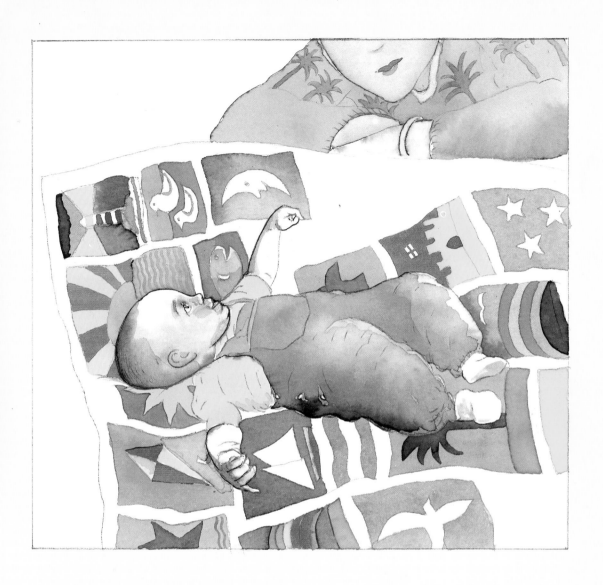

When James was a baby his mother said, "Won't it
be fun when he can walk? Then we can play with him."

When James could walk he walked across the
room and sat down and looked out of the window.
His dad said, "Won't it be fun when James can talk?
Then we can play with him."

When James could talk he said, "I want to go into the garden." He went into the garden and sat down and watched a spider spinning a web. His mother said, "Shall we play hide-and-seek?" His dad said, "Let's have a race. I bet you win."

James was watching a beetle. It was a very slow
beetle. It walked all the way up the garden path
and James followed it. Then it was five o'clock
and Mom went to make supper. Dad went to weed
the garden. There was no time for hide-and-seek
or races.

When James was three his grandma gave him some
finger paints. "Oh good!" said his mom. "Now we
can paint a great big house with flowers and trees
all around it."

James found a very thin pencil. "I am going to
draw a very small house," said James. He drew a
very small house on a very small piece of paper.

When James was four his dad bought him some
new yellow boots and a shiny coat to keep the
rain out.

"Oh good!" said Mom. "Let's go out in the rain
and wind and splash in the puddles and watch the
leaves blowing about."

James put on his boots, which squeaked, and his
coat, which creaked, and went out with Mom, but
the rain had stopped and the wind had blown
away. All the leaves were lying in piles.

James looked at them, and while he was watching
another leaf came down very quietly and lay on
top of the heap.

"That is going to be *my* leaf," said James, but just
then his mother came running along and kicked all
the leaves into the air. "Isn't this fun?" said Mom.
James looked for his leaf, but he could not see it
anymore.

On the other side of the road was a wide black
puddle like a dark looking glass. James leaned over
and saw his own face, but dark, and the dark sky
and the branches of a dark tree. It was very quiet
down there in the puddle. "I should like to live
in there," James said.

But then his mother came running up and jumped in
the puddle. Little bits of puddle flew everywhere.
"Isn't this fun?" Mom said.

James looked for his face in the puddle, and the
dark sky and the dark branches, but they had
gone. The puddle was all broken up.

When the snow came James went out with his
parents to walk in the white. "Let's make a
snowman," said Dad to Mom, so they did. James
was watching a bird with a berry under a bush.
"Let's throw snowballs," said Mom to Dad, so
they did, and the bird flew away. "Don't you want
to throw snowballs?" said Mom.

"I want to look at the snow," James said, but the
snow was full of footprints and holes, and when
Mom threw a snowball it knocked off the
snowman's head. "Let's go home," said James.

In spring the sun shone and the birds flew across
the sky. James sat in the garden and watched the
clouds float from one side of the sky to the other.

"Let's go to the park," said Mom, "and play on the swings and the slide."

"Good-bye clouds," said James. He went to the park with Mom.

Mom swung on the swings and slid on the slide
and crawled through the concrete pipes. She
climbed up the jungle gym. "Come on, James,"
Mom said. "This is fun."

James found a young caterpillar walking in the grass.

He followed the caterpillar all the way to the path.
There was a girl walking on the path. "Don't step
on my caterpillar," James said. "My name's
Paula," said the girl. "You can come for a walk
with me and my caterpillar," James said. "I've
been to play school," Paula said. "My mother
always brings me to the park after play school."

Paula's mother was swinging on the swings and sliding on the slide, just like James's mother. "Come on, Paula," said Paula's mother. "This is fun."

"What's play school like?" said James. "It's nice," said Paula. "They leave you alone." "Come on, James," said James's mother. "I'll race you home. I bet you win."

"Good-bye Paula," James said. "Good-bye caterpillar."

When they got home James said, "Mom, I want to
go to play school." "No you don't," said Mom.
"We have lots of fun at home." "I want to go to
play school." James said. "You'd rather stay at
home and have fun with Mom," said Dad.
"I want to go to play school," said James.

James went to play school. Paula was there.
"Hello James," Paula said. "This is Emma, and
this is John, and this is Steven and this is Sara."

"Hello," said James. "What do we do now?" "I'm
going to read my book," Sara said. "We are going
to play snap," said Steven and Emma. "Let's just
talk," said Paula to John. "Oh what fun!" said
James's mother. "Look, James, finger paints and a
sand tray and a rocking horse and clay and
crayons and a drum!"

James's mother rode on the rocking horse. Paula's mother painted with the finger paints. Steven's mother played with the clay. John's mother scratched in the sand tray. Emma's mother scrawled with the crayons and Sara's mother sang a loud song and banged the drum. Sara read her book. Paula talked to John. Steven and Emma played snap.

James found a very thin pencil and a very small
piece of paper. He drew a caterpillar.

"This is fun," said James.